poems and paintings by

Douglas Florian

harcourt brace & company

SAN DIEGO • NEW YORK • LONDON

in the swim

Requests for permission to make copies of any part of the
work should be mailed to: Permissions Department,
Harcourt Brace & Company, 6277 Sea Harbor Drive,
Orlando, Florida 32887-6777.

Library of Congress Cataloging-in-Publication Data
Florian, Douglas.
In the swim: poems and paintings/by Douglas Florian.
p. cm.
Summary: A collection of humorous poems about
such underwater creatures as the starfish, piranha, and clam.
ISBN 0-15-201307-5
1. Marine fauna—Juvenile poetry. 2. Children's poetry, American.
[1. Marine animals—Poetry. 2. Humorous poetry.
3. American poetry.] I. Title.
PS3556.L589I5 1997
811'.54—dc20 95-52616
First edition
A C E F D B

PRINTED IN SINGAPORE

Contents

Could do with legs!

Just think what we

Our pearly eggs.

Upstream we spawn

We somersault!

We vault!

We jump!

Our leaps astound!

We bound!

We spring!

The Salmon

The Piranhas

It's widely known
That grown piranhas
Are long on teeth
But short on manners.

The Sawfish

You'll see a saw

Upon my jaw,

But I can't cut

A two-by-four,

Or build a bed,

Or frame a door.

My splendid saw's

For goring fishes—

I eat them raw

And don't do dishes.

14

The Sea Horse

You have
No hooves.
You have no hair.
You don't eat oats.
You don't breathe air.
You hatch from eggs.
You cannot race.
(You have no legs
With which to chase.)
You're not a colt
Nor mare
Nor filly.
You're called a horse.
I call that silly.

The Whale

W i d e as a wall
And just as tall.
A wall with a tail.
A ship.
A sail.
A wharf.
A WHALE.

19

The Starfish

Although it seems
That I'm all arms,
Some other organs
Give me charm.
I have a mouth
With which to feed.
A tiny stomach
Is all I need.
And though it's true
I have no brain,
I'm still a *star*—
I can't complain.

The Ray

Grand and gray
The regal ray
Slyly g l i d e s
Upon its prey.
It almost flies
On weightless wings.
Its whiplike tail
With poison stings.
All creatures near
This royal ray
Retreat in fear:
Make way!
Make way!

The Flounders

Flat as a pancake
Flat as a crepe
Flounders are flat
As a prairie in shape.
While waiting on
Their smooth white side
Below the sand
For food they hide,
Awaiting shrimp
And smaller fishes,
These flattish, mattish
Living dishes.

The Sharks

Sharks can park
Wherever they wish.
They do not fear
The other fish.
Sharks can swim
Wherever they please.
On this each other
Fish agrees.

The Blenny

There are uglier fish than a blenny—

But not many.

The Flying Fish

We don't wish to brag or boast
But we can fly along the coast.
We don't want to rant or rave
But we can soar above a wave.
Side by side we glide and skim—
And by the way, we also swim!

The Clam

They say, "As happy as a clam,"
But would *you* like to have to cram
Your body deep inside a shell?
And furthermore: I think clams smell.

The Anglerfish

Lurking on the ocean floor
There works a crafty carnivore.
The anglerfish has set a trap
With its dangling, fleshy flap,
Complete with fishing pole and bait,
And all it has to do is wait
For some poor fish to take the lure
And make the ocean one fish fewer.

The Skates

The skinny skates are flat as plates.
They feed on small invertebrates
They find upon the ocean floor
Then skate along to find some more.

The Manatee

The manatee is not a man.
It's heavy as a minivan.
It has a bristly, big mustache,
And paddle tail to make a splash.
The manatee does not take tea.
It swallows plants beneath the sea.
It eats so much that it may seem
At times to be a manateam.

39

The Jellyfish

Thin
As a drape
Umbrella shaped,
It gently glides
Through the seascape.
Though small in size
And with no eyes
Its tentacles can paralyze.
In sporty spurts
It loves to flutter
In its vain search
For peanut
Butter.

The Oysters

Did you know the ocean's oysters
Sometimes change from girls to boysters?
Then the boys change back to girls.
(Are the girls the ones with pearls?)

The Rainbow Trout

So suave!
So chic!
So magnifique!
To sport a rainbow
On your cheek!
And down your flank!
So swell!
So swank!
Divine!
Delish!

Too bad you're a fish.

The Tetra

The itty-bitty, pretty tetra
Is small, minute, petite, et cetra.

The illustrations in this book were done in watercolor on
rough French watercolor paper.
The display type was set in Belwe Light.
The text type was set in Sabon.
Color separations by Classicscan Pte. Ltd., Singapore
Printed and bound by Tien Wah Press, Singapore
This book was printed on
totally chlorine-free Nymolla Matte Art paper.
Production supervision by Stanley Redfern
Designed by Kaelin Chappell